Napoleon Blue Books for Children

Presents

Fly Witness

written by

J. Kent Preyer

illustrated by

Tiffany Fladager

cover painting by

Amit Sadik

NAPOLEON BLUE PRESS

FLY WITNESS

J. Kent Preyer

Copyright © 2016 by J. Kent Preyer
All Rights Reserved

Published by Napoleon Blue Books for Children
A subsidiary of Napoleon Blue Press

Book Illustrations:
Copyright © 2016 by Tiffany Fladager
Cover Painting:
Copyright © 2016 by Amit Sadik
Author Photograph:
Copyright © 2016 by Robin C. Eagan

Illustration Photography: Ara Arbabzadeh

Cover Design: Sarah Wynes

Interior Book Design: J Kent Preyer

All unique fonts are used with permission
of the type designers who created them.

Published in the United States of America
First Edition 2016
Napoleon Blue Press
ISBN: 978-0-9903850-6-6

This book is dedicated to
Erin Preyer and Eric Preyer

"So come with me, where dreams are born, and time is never planned. Just think of happy things, and your heart will fly on wings, forever, in Never Never Land!"

J.M. Barrie
Peter Pan

This story may seem buggy;
Yet, every word is quite true,
And if it happened to me,
It could happen to you.

THE BEGINNING

Once upon a time...*

*Well,
actually, it was last year,
my

Showdown

began,
with my deep,
darkest, fear.

It began with my wife.
We'd been married a day;
but
the

Honeymoon

ended,

when I heard
my bride say:

"Honey...

2

...Come to the kitchen!

Quick! Quick!

Quick!

It's a fly.
It keeps buzzing,
and it's making me

Sick!"

She scowled at the rogue,
circling
the
cheese.

The moment I saw him,
I fell
to
my
knees.

I couldn't conceal it.
I could no longer hide,
my deep,

DARKEST,

FEAR,

deep,
dark,
down

inside.

6

I choked.

I whimpered.

I said,

"I... I... I...

I can't kill a bug from the earth or the sky!...

...and my worst
fear of all,

is to

MURDER

a fly."

"MURDER A FLY?

Your
brain's
come

UNSNUG!

What kind of a man is it
who won't
kill a Bug?...

...Flies are pests!
They're
grotesque!
They're a scourge
and a

CURSE;

a ghastly annoyance,
I can think of
no worse!...

...Use a swatter!
The
paper!
Use the hat off your
head! I just want that

FLY dead.

I said, dead, dead, dead...

...Dead!"

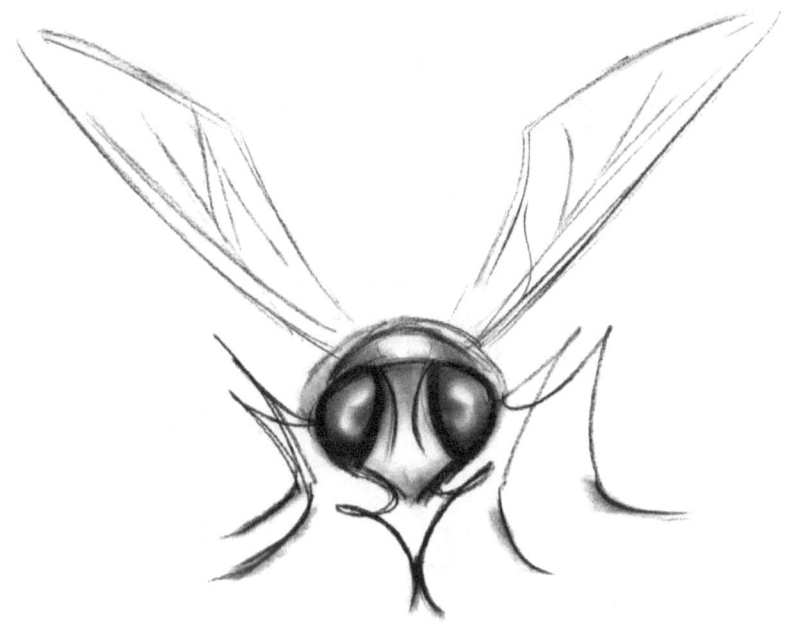

I began
shaking with frights.

My body twitched

with
strange

frets.

My wife made
some phone calls,

and

they came with the nets.

My wife spared no money.
I was sent to the best.

Dr. Shrinknoggin

is
the
best,

East coast

or West.

15

Dr. Shrinknoggin's healed thousands. She studied in France. She cured a whole town **ONCE** who feared Lava Lamps!

Dr. Shrinknoggin is brilliant.

She's as swift as can be.

She used a

HYPNO Mind-Reverse Wheel™

...and she used it on

Me!

I swirled. I twirled.
I hurled,
back through

TIME!

The
**Hypno
Mind-Reverse
Wheel**™

was controlling

my mind.

Lights flashed,
as years passed.

My brain was

TRANSFIXED.

I was 16 again...

then 10...

...and then

6.

My eyes crossed.
My head tossed.
Smoke came from my
scorching-hot ears.

Dr. Shrinknoggin
EXCLAIMED...

"We're at the root of your entomological fears!"

"Your subconscious holds the clues," she gleaned.
"It's what you see in your mind, I desire."

Then,
I saw me as a kid (when my memories got hid).
I saw **me** swinging in a tire.

I heard a
teensy bellow
from the hollow of a tree.
A voice cried,
"HELP ME!
HELP ME!
HELP ME!"
So...
I went to look and see.

There, I saw
a fly TRAPPED,
all wrapped in web gauze.

Poised to pounce
was a spider,

with FlY Sauce

in
IT's
claws.

I was chomping a

JUICY gum wad,

(that I keep on
the post of my bed).

In a flash
I spit it like a rocket,
on that spider's hairy,

HAIR-RAISING

head!

I searched through my
pockets; grabbed a
TOOTSIE POP
(only half licked).

"Climb aboard!"
I
implored
him.

And that fly did,
lickety split.

He licked
      his little broken legs;
cleared a **TEARDROP**
            from his eye.
I felt a little proud,
that I'd saved the
            little guy.

Dr. Shrinknoggin
            interrupted.
I think she had a hunch:
"If you hurry up **your** story,
we could wrap this up by lunch."

So...

the tree and the fly,
faded

clean away,

and
I harkened back
to what happened,

at the end of that

LONG AGO

day.

I was all tucked in bed;
Mommy turning off
MY LIGHT.
She whispered in my
sleepy ear,

"Don't let the
bed bugs
bite."

The next thing I remember
in my little six-year head,
I was wrapped and tied in

Blanky,

and

rolling

off

my

bed!

KID...

...NAPPED!

...**TAKEN HOSTAGE!**
like a prisoner of
SOME WAR!

Teensy voices yipped:

"**WE'VE**

GOT

HIM!"

...then,

they

lugged

me

OUT

my

DOOR!

Off the porch,

through the yard,

...into THE

WOODS

I was lifted,

taken

to

the

STRANGEST place,

I never knew existed!

There were **HOUSES AND STREETS,** like you would see in any city, but everything here I saw, was

little itty

bitty.

Then,
I noticed my captors
were of the insect sort,
and a

SHERIFF BEE

said, **"HEY YOU!"**

to me.

"We're taking you
to COURT...

...We're arresting you for murder,

on **67** counts.

If found guilty of these charges **SON**, your head is gonna

BOUNCE!"

He spoke!

But
more
FREAKY?
was
the
size of
that bee!

I was no bigger than he;
he, no bigger than me!

I saw posters posted on trees, like when we lost our dog, TREVOR; but these posters were of me, (and they said)

WANTED

DEAD

OR

WHATEVER.

To the courthouse
we went. They swore
in jurors quite deftly.
They
were
12
Angry
Bugs,
and their looks were
quite deathly.

My **CRICKET** attorney stood up and proclaimed, "My client's **NOT** guilty! He's **CLEARLY** insane!"

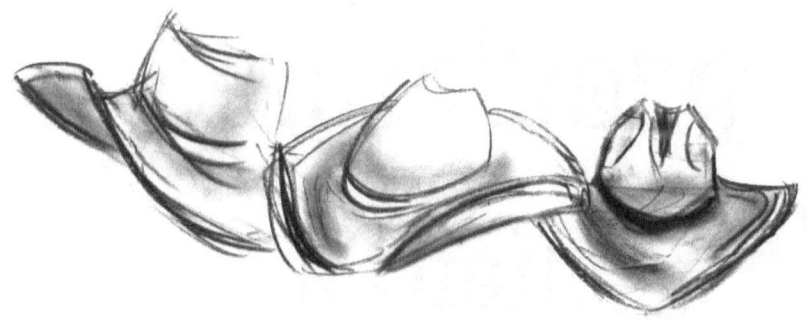

The Walking Stick Gang were up to no good!

They wore RAWHIDES AND RIFLES, just like CLINT EASTWOOD.

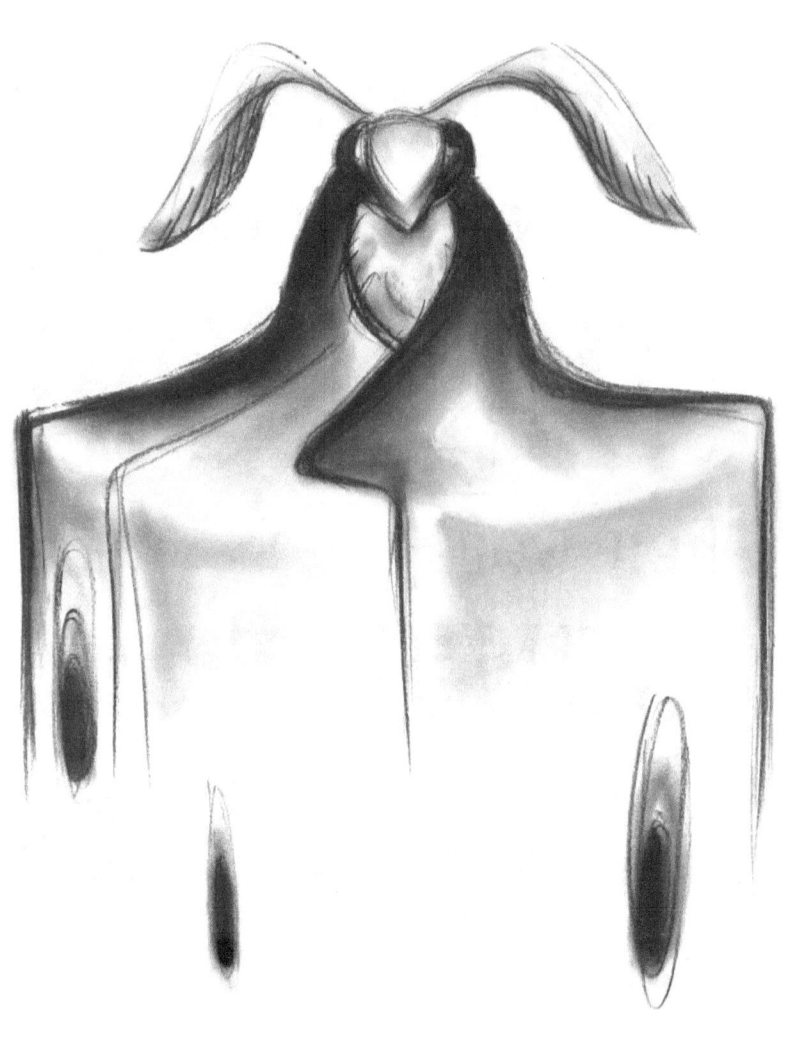

JUDGE MOTH

told the crowd,

"Now,
  put away your guns...

We're not shooting

any **BOY**

tonight!

...unless, of course,

he runs."

"I'm not the guy you want!"
I yelled!
"I'm just a kid,
CAN'T YOU
SEE?"

Then some lady called out,
"HE'S THE ONE!"
and she pointed
her pincer at me!

"He's the one who did it!" the pretty, young LADY BUG charged.

"He burned up my house and my children, when he BURNED UP those leaves in his yard."

Next,
came more witnesses,
all spilling their GUTS,
...and I was
the culprit,
no
IFS,
ands,
or buts.

Grasshoppers, weevils, dragonflies, fleas; every size, and SHAPE, COLOR of bug there can be!...

...and like
birds of a feather,
they all rallied together,
in a chorus of abhorrence

for **me!**

"DUNG BALL'S
BABE ROOT
was
Hill Hollow's
Favorite Son,
'til
he was shot dead at
WIGGLY
FIELD
by your
Red Ryder BB Gun."

55

"The Lightning BugZenskis'

SKY SHOW

made our summer nights
magically glow.
Now, the Bugzenskis
are
dead,
in a jar by your bed,
because you didn't even
think to punch holes."

56

"Governor Cootie declared

GRUBVILLE

a

carnage

COMPLETE,

when you left your

Slip-N-Slide on

for nearly one week!"

"It was at SMORGASBORD PARK, in front of my eyes, when my Auntie Anne Ant met her DEMISE...

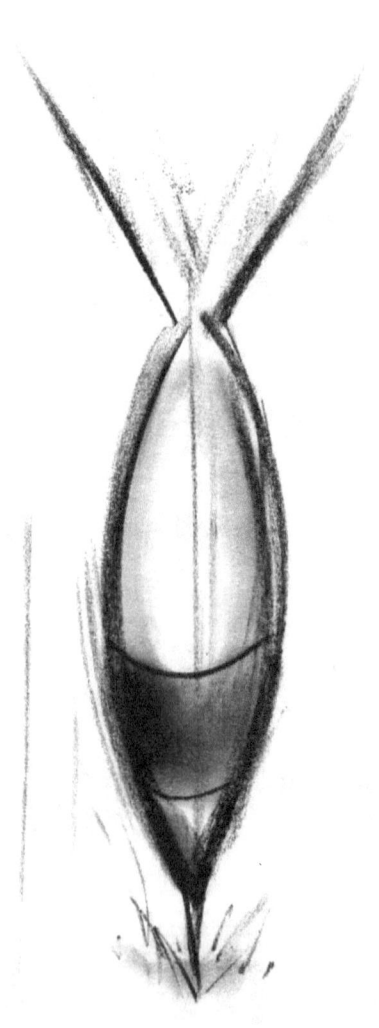

...'Oh, heaven
help me!'
were the last words
she said,
when that boy's
LAWN DART
fell
right
on
her
head!"

Ralph the Roach was **QUITE COCKY** when he took the stand.

Wiping the sweat from his forehead, his **CHILLING STORY** began...

"...This **boy** runs a **MOTEL** OF **HORROR** out on lonely old **ROUTE 62**. They say you **CHECK IN**, but never **CHECK OUT**, because the beds are made of **GLUE!**"

"THE ROLY-POLY POM-PON TEAM

brought cheer to every sports game! ...then your **magnifying glass,** reduced them to ash, and I say,

shame!

Shame!

Shame!"

"The death of the rock band

THE
BEATLE
BUGS

is a remembrance dark and miserable. You pogo-sticked on their tour bus, and now they sing with The Choir Invisible."

"The Slug Kids slid out of their beds, CHRISTMAS MORNING; put on their snow boots, grabbed their sleds; HEARTS WERE SOARING!...

...but the

Snowflakes

a falling,
               made the
CORONER come calling.

This boy was pouring

Salt

on their heads!"

My accusers kept on **ACCUSING,** and their stories grew more gruesome.

My attorney joined the mob outside, chanting:

"NOOSE HIM!

NOOSE HIM!

NOOSE HIM!"

insecticide
was my charge;
A MASS-KILLER FOR KICKS!

I would be tried and
hung by a lynch-mob,

and

I

was

only

SIX.

Dr. Shrinknoggin

reassured me:
"This happened long,
long **AGO.**"

Then she mumbled aloud
about a **BOOK TOUR,**
and how we'd be on every
TV Talk Show!

"A stellar **END** is what we need," she mused. "Then **The Pulitzer** will be **mine** for the winning." She spun the

Hypno
Mind-Reverse
Wheel™
once
more,

and back to my bug trial I went spinning.

Said **JUDGE MOTH**
to
the Jury,
"Is the decree
YEA or **NAY?**"

as Miss Mapleleaf,
the Mantis, bowed her
head down to pray.

74

Then the courtroom doors flew open. The crowd **scuttled** out of the way; and a fly shuffled in on six crutches, crying,

"**WAIT! i HAVE SOMETHING TO SAY!**"

He looked fragile
and
small,
as he hopped
up to
the
stand.

Then he swore on
the **BUG BIBLE**, with
his tiny fly hand.

"It was the **BLACK WIDOW WITCH** from **DARK VALLEY OF DEAD!**

I was wrapped and ready for feasting, in the grip of her **SINISTER WEB...**

...When this boy came along, I had no hope,

only

doom...

...Then he sealed up the

WIDOW
WITCH

in a

Double-Bubble-Gum

tomb...

...Like a heaven
sent

KNIGHT,

his fears all ignored,
he **swooped** in
and saved me,
with his shiny

RED SWORD...

...You're all mad as **hornets**, but if you LET YOUR HEARTS SEE, this boy should be honored, not hung from a tree!"

The town was left
SPEECHLESS;

every
bug,
BIG
and
small.

That brave little fly
had silenced them all.

I
stared
out at that crowd,
and I was
not proud.

HOW COULD BUGS

FORGIVE

SOMEONE

LIKE...

...but they started to

cheer!

though...

"Hail the

BOY HERO!"

"Set him free!"

"Set him free!"

"Set him free!"

Then...

...there was a

BIG BUG CELEBRATION!

That's where it all ends.
And, the fly,

HE and I,

became

best of friends.

So, my deep,
darkest, fear,
wasn't **FEAR**,
not at all!
I felt **LOVE**
for my friends
that fly...

...and that crawl.

Now, the Doc has her

BOOK TOUR...

...and I have

my

Wife...

...and all our bugs
live in

peace,

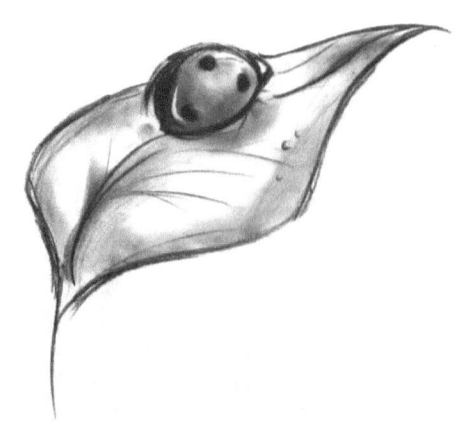

because

a FLY

saved

my

life.

THE END

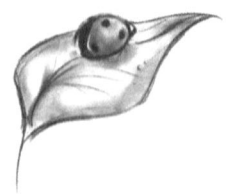

If you read this in Paris,
Acapulco, or Kalamazoo...

...at the beach, on Mars,
or in a cage at the zoo...

I say, thank you, gracias,
danke, and merci boucoup!

And if you had a smile... a
giggle... or a chortle or two,

Could you spread the word,
and please write a review?

Amazon.com
Goodreads.com
Barnesandnoble.com
Your favorite blog

Or wherever you enjoy books...

ABOUT THE AUTHOR

Photo © 2016 Robin C. Eagan

J. Kent Preyer was born and raised in Southern Missouri. He now lives in Northern California, where all his bugs live in PEACE.

FLY WITNESS is his second book. His first novel is the highly acclaimed Southern Romantic Comedy, TENNESSEE WILDFLOWERS.

www.jkentpreyer.com

J. Kent Preyer Author

ABOUT THE ARTISTS

ILLUSTRATOR

Tiffany Fladager has been drawing, designing and creating since she could pick up a pencil. Her artistic passion lies in the ever evolving world of animation and film, as well as illustration and graphic design. Her talent has taken her to Paros, Greece, where she studied with the esteemed Aegean School of the Arts. Her provocative and realistic pieces are inspired from movement, emotion, music and dance.

COVER DESIGN

Sarah Wynes is a professional graphic designer and the owner of Click Graphic Design Solutions in Northern California. She creates an experience as she combines visual elements and typography to clearly communicate a message. Sarah is also a talented outdoor photographer.

COVER PAINTING

Amit Sadik is a gifted artist residing in Israel. His visually striking paintings evoke imaginative, fantastic worlds that often appear supernatural. His art is achieved through use of traditional and modern artistic techniques. More of his beautiful, ethereal artwork is available at:

www.AmitSadik.com

f Amit Sadik – Digital Paintings

Enjoy the deliriously fun

Audio Book

of

FLY WITNESS

Narrated by

Dan Jones

Audible.com

Amazon.com

iTunes

www.ingramcontent.com/pod-product-compliance
Lightning Source LLC
Chambersburg PA
CBHW020151180626
46810CB00004B/1844